P9-CLJ-754

Goodnight Stories from the Big Tree

with more than 50 tales for bedtime

told by
Laura Magni

illustrated by
Giulia Orecchia

translation by
Colin Clark

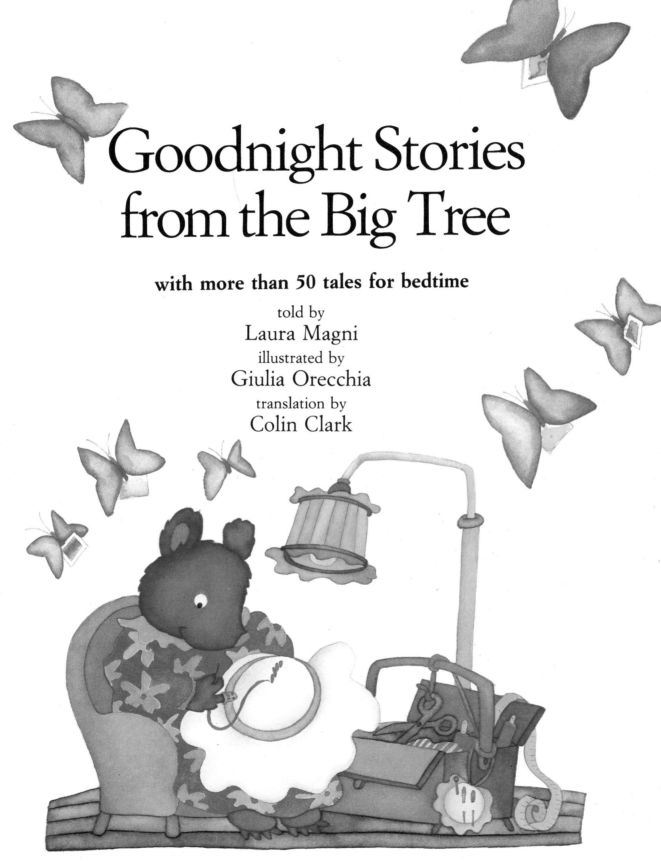

DERRYDALE BOOKS
New York

© 1989 HAPPY BOOKS, Milan, Italy
This 1990 edition published by Derrydale Books
distributed by Crown Publishers, Inc., 225 Park Avenue South,
New York, New York 10003
Printed in Italy
ISBN 0-517-69687-8
hgfedeba

The Big Tree and the Wind Flowers

From time to time, the wind blew over the Big Tree. Sometimes the wind came from the distant sea, but more often it came carrying the smells of hills and forests. On one very special day, the wind blew so hard that the clouds seemed to be galloping across the sky like dark, angry horses. The smells in that wind were of far distant prairies and deserts, mountains and rivers.

But the wind was tired out after its long journey. It blew strongly all morning, but in the afternoon it died away to a gentle breeze. Then, all the twigs and leaves and seeds that had been swept up and carried along by the wind began to drift down to the ground all around the Big Tree.

One of the seeds fell into a plant pot that Sandy Squirrel had out on his balcony. Sandy liked to have shrubs and flowers on the balcony where he would sit in the evening after a day of nut-hunting.

The seed burrowed its way into the good earth in the flower pot and a few weeks later little green

shoots began to appear. Sandy watered the young plant and he was amazed and delighted when, after a few more weeks, he had some beautiful new flowers on his balcony.

Neither Sandy nor his Big Tree neighbors had ever seen anything like it before. Louisa Lizard, who was very emotional, began to cry when she saw it because she thought it was so lovely. Oscar

Owl took a photograph of it. Only Cathy Crow pretended she was not impressed. She said she'd seen more beautiful flowers on one of her overseas vacations.

Sandy was so happy. He took lots of cuttings from the wonderful plant, put them into pots, and gave one to each of his neighbors. And the Big Tree was the only tree in the woods covered with flowers that the wind had brought from so far away, the 'wind flowers' as Sandy called them.

In all the apartments in the Big Tree, from the basement right up to the penthouse, everyone was talking about the exciting news. A visitor was coming from Africa, someone who had been born in the Big Tree, but had left it at a very early age. Ossie Ostrich was returning home for a visit.

Ossie's father had been an engineer, famous for designing the strongest dams for beavers and for otters. Because of his work, his family had gone with him to many far away parts of the world.

To reach the Big Tree, Ossie was going to have to make a long journey. First of all, he had to spend days on the famous train, 'The Forest Express'; then weeks on the swamp boat, 'The Quagmire Queen'. Nobody knew how Ossie was going to make the last part of the journey, and, what was worse, nobody had any idea what he looked like. The only photograph of Ossie that remained at the Big Tree was taken when he was still inside his egg!

Ossie's visit was the event of the year because

the Big Tree had very few foreign visitors, and it was also said that Ossie was very rich and famous. But it was not easy to plan a big welcome for him since no one knew where or how he would arrive.

The Mice and the Goldfish decided to wait at the railroad station, and greet Ossie Ostrich with baskets of roasted meats, cheeses, and lettuce.

The Worms went with the Hare brothers and

Louisa Lizard to the little jetty on the pond.

Fiona Fox, the Ants and the Bears decided to

wait for Ossie at the airport, carrying bunches of ferns tied with blue ribbons.

Sandy Squirrel and the Moles thought he might be coming by bus, so they took some strawberry wine with them and waited by the highway.

Cathy Crow did not wait anywhere. She flew home in a huff, because nobody had time for her.

Only Oliver Owl stayed behind in the Big Tree. As he was awake at night, he slept during the day.

The sun was high when a beautiful balloon began to descend slowly out of the blue sky towards the silent, deserted Tree. The balloon was decorated in all the colors of the rainbow, and gleamed

in the sun. It floated down, barely brushing the tree tops, and landed in the meadow.

Wearing an elegant top hat, Ossie Ostrich climbed out of the basket beneath the balloon and looked around. There was no one in sight. Now Ossie was a very busy ostrich, who had a successful career as 'Mr. Marvel, the Hot Air Balloonist'. He waited, and he waited, and he waited! After an hour or so, as there was still no one to be seen, he decided to go away again and take care of important business somewhere else. So he hailed a yellow taxi that was passing by and left the woods.

When the Big Tree folk finally returned home, the only trace of their foreign visitor was the balloon, with the initials MM printed on it.

Tommy Toad and the Cuckoo Clock

Tommy Toad was the woodland watchmaker. His workshop was in one of the ground-level apartments in the Big Tree, and he always had lots of customers because he was so clever at repairing all kinds of timepieces.

When the Worms' waterproof watch started to make gurgling noises, Tommy was able to dry it out and give it back to them as good as new. When the Ants' kitchen clock began to go slow, causing Mrs. Ant to be late with the family supper, Tommy soon had it working again at the right speed. And when Howard Hare's grandfather clock actually started giggling like a child, a drop of Tommy's special oil made it chime again in a more dignified way.

One morning, Tommy was surprised to find a cuckoo waiting to see him in his workshop.

"Can I help you?" he asked the bird.

"I hope so," replied the cuckoo. "I'm not well."

"Don't you think you ought to go and see a bird doctor," said Tommy. "I'm only good at mending clocks and watches."

"But I'm a cuckoo clock," said the bird, hopping about nervously. "Only I can't cuckoo any more, and if I can't get my cuckoo back, I'll be out of a job."

"How long is it since you lost your cuckoo?" asked Tommy.

"About two weeks ago," sighed the cuckoo clock. "I remember I was very busy. Every day I was asked to fly past and tell someone when it was nine o'clock, or ten o'clock, or twelve o'clock. If anyone from the Big Tree was outside in the woods, I was supposed to let them know the time. It was exhausting, but now nobody wants me anymore, because I can't cuckoo."

The poor bird began to snivel.

"Now then, pull yourself together," said Tommy briskly. "Let me have a look at you." He peered at the bird through a magnifying glass. He looked carefully at his feathers and at his feet, under his wings and down his throat, to see if there was any sign which would show him what the trouble was. But he could find nothing wrong.

"Everything seems to be working properly," said Tommy at last. "I think it's just that your cuckoo is worn out from overwork. It needs a vacation. Why don't you fly off somewhere for a

couple of weeks away from the Big Tree. If you don't use your cuckoo for a while, I'm sure it will work again as well as ever."

And the cuckoo-clock did what Tommy told him, packed his bags and flew away for a fortnight by the sea. There he perched all day in the sun, and slept late every morning and never told anyone the time once during the whole vacation.

Then the cuckoo-clock flew back to the Big Tree. And at noon on the day after his return, he hopped out on to the branch beside his front door, opened his beak and announced the time with the twelve loudest cuckoos ever heard.

The Big Tree cuckoo-clock was back in business, as good as new.

Fiona Fox's troubles began when Louisa Lizard moved into the apartment above. Louisa was not a bad neighbor, but she did have one very unfortunate habit. She loved sad films, and Louisa would spend hours every evening sobbing before the TV.

When one of her favorites was showing, like 'You Weep and I'll Wail,' or 'All Moan Together,' Louisa would immediately start to cry.

Fiona would not have minded, only the sad films always seemed to begin just as Louisa was running a bath. And she always forgot to turn off the taps. Night after night, Fiona found herself sitting at her desk downstairs, typing her great novel, while drops of water fell on her from overhead.

Fiona complained to Louisa about it, and she promised to turn off the water next time before watching television, but always she forgot.

Fiona was really despairing when Mr. Worm,

the Big Tree's best gardener, proposed a way out.

"Your desk is the same size as Louisa's bath," said Mr. Worm. "If you place it just underneath the bath, and cover the desk-top with earth and seeds, you'll be able to grow a lovely garden."

Fiona followed Mr. Worm's advice. From then on, during the daytime Fiona would type away at her desk, surrounded by flowers as if she were out in the country. And, in the evenings, she would just put an umbrella over herself and her typewriter, and carry on working, as her beautiful desk-top garden was watered by the drops from the ceiling.

Babs and Bruce Bear were a hard-working couple. They had a family laundry business in the Big Tree, and while Babs took care of the washing, and cleaning, and ironing, Bruce was kept busy collecting dirty clothes and delivering clean clothes all over the woods. Their laundry business prospered, but they never seemed to be able to take any time off. The other Big Tree residents could not remember having seen either of them in anything but their working clothes. Bruce wore a pair of blue dungarees for making the deliveries, and Babs had a plain, gray dress that had become her uniform.

One afternoon, Bruce brought an especially mixed bag of clothes back to the laundry. There were ear-muffs to be washed for the rabbits who had earache. There were the moles' cushion covers to be repaired. They always needed sewing because moles make holes everywhere. And there were very small overcoats to be pressed for the ants, with all their tiny folds and tucks which were so hard to iron.

Amongst all the other clothes, there was also a lovely evening dress for cleaning. It was made of silk and was a 'Spring-beginning-in-the-woods' green color. When she set eyes on it, Babs just could not resist trying it on. It was a bit big for her around the tail, but she tied it with a wild buttercup. Then, after admiring her reflection in the glass door of a washing machine, Babs found a long, violet, velvet ribbon and tied it round her

head. She thought that she looked just great!

At that moment, the phone rang. "Hi there, Babs!" It was the voice of the young owl from the attic apartment. "We're having a surprise come-as-you-are party. You've to come up here at once, dressed just the way you are. It'll be great fun."

Babs Bear was delighted! She left her washing machine and her ironing board and ran upstairs as quickly as she could. The door to the Owl family's house was wide open. Walter Woodpecker was there, wearing a bathrobe. Louisa Lizard had her tail wrapped in a mudpack. The Mouse children were all wearing rubber gloves because they'd been washing the dishes when the phone rang.

When Babs Bear came in, all the chattering stopped. Everyone was amazed at how pretty she looked. When her husband, Bruce, arrived in his dungarees he also thought she was beautiful. In fact, he decided then and there that it was about time that they had a night out to enjoy themselves. What was the point of all their hard work if they never had any fun together?

And so, the next day they bought themselves some fancy clothes, and in the evening they went to 'The Moonlight', the popular night club. And there they danced the night away, just as they had done when they were both young and carefree.

Olga Makes Her Dream Come True

Olga the Owl's big ambition was to sing on television. She had a very musical hoot and everyone in the Big Tree loved hearing her sing all the latest hits. But she had her dream, that at least once in her life she'd be on TV! Unfortunately, she did not know anyone who worked in television. It seemed that she would never fulfil her ambition, that it would remain just a dream.

But her husband, Oliver Owl, was determined to help make Olga's dream come true. Although he was a night watchman by profession, he was also a very keen photographer. He knew how happy Olga would be if only he could take a picture of her singing on television. She could frame it and keep it to remind her of her big moment!

So, with the help of Walter Woodpecker, the Owls set to work. They got an old television set from the Cat family. They took out the insides and just kept the front and the screen. Then they borrowed Dr. Mole's electric razor, which looked like a television microphone. Finally, they hung on the wall a big curtain with palm trees painted on it.

Olga Owl put on her best dress, and put round her neck her best string of pearls. She stood in front of the curtain and began to sing into the electric razor, while Walter held the frame of the television set in front of her. At just that moment, Oliver took a color photo of her. When it was printed, there was Olga Owl singing on TV!

The Mouse family were early risers. They always had been, all five of them. No matter how early the Big Tree residents rose in the morning, they could always find traces of mice about, because they had been there first.

To wake themselves up, the Mouse family used a special kind of alarm clock. They had five of them, one for each mouse. Before going to bed at night, the whole family agreed on the wake-up time for next morning. Then each Mouse set an alarm clock, so that, at the right time, instead of ringing a bell, a strong smell of cheese was released. It was the most effective way possible to get the mice out of their beds!

Each Mouse had their own favorite cheese, so from one alarm clock came the smell of Cheddar, and from another the smell of Danish Blue: one gave off the smell of Limburger, another Gorgonzola. The early morning air in the Mouse household was unbelievable!

On this particular morning, everyone was up even earlier than usual. They were all excited,

"Hurry up," Mrs. Mouse told the children. "Be sure to clean your teeth properly, or you won't be able to eat your cheese when you're older!"

Actually, they all had teeth that were perfect for eating cheese, but they did as they were told, because they didn't want to lose their cheese-eating skills later on.

Mr. Mouse was ready and waiting. He had combed his whiskers neatly and drunk his morning cup of barley juice. Then he had eaten a dish of barley flakes and finished breakfast with a few barley cookies. Mr. Mouse was very fond of barley. Now he was nervously scampering about the apartment, waiting for the arrival of an important visitor.

The Mouse family were expecting none other than the rich Countess Crow, who lived in a luxury penthouse in the topmost branch. It was rumored that she was descended from an old Crow family in a distant part of the woods, and that her father had

been the notorious Lord Jim Crow, who, many years ago, had frightened the tail feathers off many a young pigeon living near the Big Tree.

Countess Crow, as everyone respectfully called her, had a magnificent apartment to which only the best Big Tree residents were ever invited. The Mouse family had only seen her in the distance, but the fame of Monty Mouse, the father, had evidently reached the penthouse. He was a very fine tailor, who had once had his picture in the Big Tree Gazette, when he had made a special belt-and-suspender combination for the President of the Woodlands Congress, a very nervous rat.

Yesterday evening, Countess Crow had sent

Monty a note, asking for an appointment next morning 'to discuss an exclusive design.'

Late into the night Monty Mouse had worked, surrounded by his wife and children, who plied him with suggestions, encouragement and barley coffee, designing model after model: evening dresses, morning dresses, dance dresses, dresses for the rain, and even dresses for walking on

clouds: the countess often did this. All were lovely. All were 'exclusive designs'!

At the appointed hour, the doorbell suddenly

gave off an aroma of Parmesan cheese. Beside
themselves with excitement, the whole Mouse
family stood in a row behind a small mountain of
drawings and sample pieces of material.

"Good day," said the Countess when the door
was opened. She stepped back. "I won't come in,
if you don't mind. I feel rather queasy. I'd better
stay out in the fresh air. Have you an exclusive design for me?"

One by one, the Mouse family handed the designs to the Countess, and, one by one, she threw
them back through the door with. Finally she said
crossly: "There isn't one here!"

"But surely you like something?" squeaked Monty Mouse. "Isn't there one you could wear?"

"Why on earth would I want to wear it?" exclaimed the Countess. "I want something for the floor of my porch!"

She took a deep breath and stepped inside the front door. The Mouse family were astonished.

"You see," said Countess Crow, "you can't fly. Some of my best friends can't either. But you all have this untidy habit of walking, crawling or hopping about, and that leaves my front porch covered in footprints or pawprints, and so on. I need a large rug, but it must be an exclusive design."

The Countess turned to the Mouse family, but they had all fainted with shock, except for Mona Mouse, who was the most practical daughter.

"Tell your father to bring me some exclusive designs for a doormat this evening. If I like one, he can make it up for me." And she swept out of the house in a swirl of feathers.

So, when Mona had revived her family with pieces of over-ripe cheese, Monty Mouse set about designing something exclusive for Catriona Crow's porch. Fortunately, she was delighted with one special pattern and Monty made it up for her.

Afterwards, on his front window, Monty printed the words: *By appointment – Exclusive Designer for the Countess Crow.*

When an Owl has a Goldfish for a Friend

It is not often that a friendship blossoms between birds and fish, but it happened at the Big Tree play-school. The young Owls and the Goldfish from the nearby stream got along very well together. It was not exactly love at first sight. It was difficult to get any sight of the young goldfish at all, because on dry land they had to wear a breathing mask and carry a tank of water on their backs. But the Owls soon realized that even though the Goldfish looked different, they were just as much fun to be with as the little Mice or Rabbits or Cats. And once they accepted that it was no use expecting the Goldfish to run around the playground, the Owls had some good games of catch with them.

But, the older Owls and the older Goldfish had never met. After all, Owls and Goldfish usually move in completely different circles. But the young Owls pestered their parents so much that at last an invitation was issued for the Goldfish family to come and visit the Owls one afternoon for coffee and cookies. The Goldfish accepted the invitation, a little nervously because they were afraid they might be a bit uncomfortable in the Owls' home.

Ma and Pa Owl put on their aprons and cleaned the house until it shined like a new pin. They made the young Owls polish their beaks and scrub their talons. Then they all waited for their guests to come.

It was a bit awkward at first when the Goldfish came in. It was no problem taking the gifts they were carrying, but it is not easy for an Owl to shake 'hands' with a Goldfish – wings and fins don't go together very easily. And there was an embarrassing moment when the two mothers tried to kiss each other and Mrs. Owl's beak bounced off Mrs. Goldfish's face mask.

Once the Goldfish discovered that the Owls had a real bath in their house, everything became more relaxed. The Goldfish had no need of a bath where they lived, but all the youngsters went into the Owls' bathroom, and in no time at all there was water and soap bubbles everywhere. The parents rushed in to see what was happening, and found the two young Owls and the two young

Goldfish splashing away together. At first, they were shocked, but they all began to laugh when they saw how much fun they were having.

When the games were over, the adults, and the children, cleaned up all the mess. Then the young Goldfish put their masks back on, and, amidst good wishes, the Owl family said farewell to their guests.

The following week, the Goldfish had the Owls to visit them in the stream. After that, the families were inseparable.

Sandy was the most unusual squirrel in the entire woods. He wore glasses with bright blue frames, he could make the most delicious apple and raisin tarts, and he was an artist by profession. He painted pictures for all the children. Sometimes he used a proper paint brush and sometimes he used his own tail instead, dipping it into paints made out of strawberry or blackberry juice.

He painted portraits of his friends, and, if they asked him nicely, he would also cover their walls with pictures of long, white beaches, or fields of tall grass, or snow-covered mountain tops. All the folk agreed that Sandy was very artistic.

But Sandy was a frustrated squirrel, because he had never painted a picture of himself. He had tried and tried to paint a self-portrait, always without success. There was something wrong with all the pictures. He had even tried painting himself onto a mirror, following the contours of his face, his body and his bushy tail but the result just was not right.

Sandy was tearful because he could not paint a picture of himself and his spirits were very low. His friends noticed his unhappiness and began sending him little presents to make him happy again. They sent walnut cakes, woolen scarves, and new tubes of paint. Sandy put all these gifts in a heap on the white rug in his bedroom, and just stayed right on being miserable.

Then, one night, as he lay in bed, he felt thirsty. He got up to get a nice drink of nut juice and fell

over the heap of presents. He had forgotten they were there. When he got to his feet and put on his glasses, Sandy was very surprised to find that the bedroom rug had a picture of a squirrel on it. The colors had been squeezed out of the tubes of

paint, the eyes were made from walnut cakes, and the tail was a woolly scarf. It was a perfect portrait of himself made out of the gifts from the friends who loved him!

The Hares' Computer Games

Hyram and Howard Hare were brothers. They were just like all the other hares in the woods, except that Hyram had extra large ears, and Howard, or Howie as Hyram always called him, had extra large front teeth.

When he was younger, Hyram had dreamed of being the Big Tree toboggan racing champion. But if he wanted to take part in the championships on the snow-covered hill near the Big Tree, then he had to wear a safety helmet. But Hyram just couldn't get his ears into the helmet. He folded his ears over his head, he tried rolling them up, he flattened them out. But it was all no use. His ears were too big and he couldn't take part in races.

As for Howie, when he was younger he had dreamed of being a famous TV star so that he could advertise White Gnasher Toothpaste. Howie loved this toothpaste because it was carrot flavored. But even for a toothpaste commercial, Howie's teeth were too big. They filled the screen and left no room for the brush and paste.

And so, the Hare brothers had to accept their fate. They gave up their impossible dreams, and decided instead that they would find a way to be successful, even with extra large ears and teeth.

They had a home computer which they played with all the time. They were very clever at inventing games to play on it. So Hyram lay on the floor in front of the computer and drew across the

screen a row of hares with really big ears.

"They look like fun," he said. Then it was Howie's turn and he drew on the screen a row of hares with really big teeth.

"Now we've got two teams," he said.

Then the two brothers worked out a Dungeons and Hares Adventure Game. They played it on the computer again and again. Sometimes the Ears won the Magic Carrot, and sometimes the Teeth.

And that was how the Hare brothers began their successful career as computer games' inventors. They made copies of Dungeons and Hares for all their friends at the Big Tree. Then they told all *their* friends about it, and soon the Hares were being asked to invent games for bears and mice, and worms and everyone. Eventually, the Hare brothers opened their very own computer games store on the second story of the Big Tree.

Grandpa Owl Puts Away His Nightcap

Grandpa Owl was the oldest owl in the woods. No one, even Grandpa Owl himself, knew how old he was. He was *really* old. He could not go night-flying any more with the other owls, but he was a familiar sight to the other Big Tree folk as he walked slowly around in the evening air, reading his newspaper 'The Owls' Oracle.'

He always had a long, old-fashioned nightcap on his head, because where all the other owls had a fine head of feathers, poor Grandpa had none – he was bald. When asked what had happened to his head feathers, Grandpa would say he had been frightened by a Bald Eagle, but everyone thought he was just joking.

Betsy, the Bears' young cub, would spend hours at the Owls' house, playing with the owlets. She was a very imaginative little bear. One afternoon, Grandpa Owl was dozing in his rocking chair and his nightcap slipped off his head. Betsy stood behind the old owl and noticed that his bald head shone in the light. It was just like a magic mirror. Everything in the room was reflected in it and if she stood close, Betsy could even see her own face.

When Grandpa Owl woke up, Betsy told him about the reflections on his head. He was pleased that his bald head could be so interesting. From then on, he never wore his nightcap again, because he thought everyone in the Big Tree ought to see his 'magic mirror'.

The Hares and the Racing Ants

Hyram and Howard Hare's computer games store in the Big Tree was a great success. One day a letter arrived at the store from Larry Leveret, president of the Leveret Computer Corporation. He was coming the next day and he wanted to see a completely new computer game.

When they read the letter, Hyram and Howie looked at each other in delight and dismay. They were delighted that someone so important was coming to see them. They were dismayed because they had just invented a wonderful game, called Racing Ants, but not yet written the program.

Then the Hares had a bright idea. They rushed round to see Annie Ant. When they explained what they wanted, Annie gathered all the other Ants together. Hyram and Howie divided them into two teams, a red team and a green team. Then Annie put a blob of red paint on the backs of the ants in one team, and a blob of green paint on the others. They spent the rest of the day practicing.

The next day when the great man arrived, he was shown into the store. There was a big table in the room. Hyram and Howard explained that they were going to show him the game, not on a screen, but in a real, live demonstration.

So Larry Leveret watched as the Hares called out the instruction and the two teams of ants raced back and forth across the table top. At the end he was so impressed he asked the Hares to become official games inventors for his corporation, and the Ants to be the official demonstrators.

Short-sighted Mina Mole

Most moles are short-sighted. They don't need to see very far when they are digging tunnels under the ground. Mina Mole, though, was very short sighted indeed and kept making terrible mistakes because she couldn't see at all well.

She tried to eat the bath sponge because she thought it was a piece of cheese with holes in it. She tried to drink her tea out of the tea strainer, and it spilled all over her dress. She even tried to read her book when she was holding it upside down.

The optician, who was also a mole, gave her a pair of glasses, but they got in the way when she was digging so she couldn't wear them. Eventually she was fitted with a pair of contact lenses and then she could see perfectly.

After that, because she was able to see herself properly at last, Mina spent a lot of time in front of a mirror, admiring herself and thinking what a pretty mole she was. And she became a regular customer at Louisa Lizard's beauty parlor, where she would try new kinds of lipstick and put on false eyelashes in an effort to make herself the prettiest mole in the Big Tree.

Not far away from the Big Tree, there was a little pond, and there, in a pretty little house made of rushes, lived the Duck sisters, Daphne and Dinah. Although they were not twins, the sisters looked a lot like each other, and people who didn't know them could only tell them apart by looking at the tips of their beaks. Daphne had a little brown spot, and Dinah had none.

Their best friend was Walter Woodpecker, who had an apartment at the top of the Big Tree. He was only allowed to live there on condition that he did his woodpecking somewhere else. The other residents didn't want the Big Tree to come crashing down as a result of Walter's pecking!

Walter often visited Daphne and Dinah. He felt at home with them, and he loved Daphne's herb tea. It made him feel great. Dinah also had a good effect on him because she was very good at book keeping, and Walter was terrible at addition and subtraction and could not keep his books balanced. Dinah fixed them with her calculator.

On one day, while eating a piece of Daphne's nettle pie – she was a good cook also – Walter started to cry. Dinah asked what was wrong.

"I've lost my job as the Big Tree milk and egg delivery man." Walter explained, sniffing sadly. "I can't resist pecking things because that's my na-

ture, and people have been complaining about their milk cartons being full of holes and their eggs being cracked open. Now I don't know what I'm going to do to pass the time."

The Duck sisters tried to cheer him up, but without success. He left them, still unhappy.

After he had gone, the Ducks had a good idea. They invited Walter and lots of their friends to a special party. They told everyone – except Walter, of course – to bring with them something made of leather, like a belt, or a strap, or a briefcase.

And so, the next night, when Walter arrived at the Ducks' house, there were the Snipe twins, Sally and Sandra, Mr. and Mrs. Oliver Owl, the elegant Cathy Crow, accompanied by Hyram Hare, and many others from the Big Tree. And they had all brought with them things made out of leather that needed extra holes put in them.

"Please, Walter," said Cathy Crow. "You have such a sharp beak, punch another hole in my belt – it's too loose."

"Walter, please put a hole in the new strap for my briefcase," said Oliver Owl.

Everyone wanted to make use of Walter's talent as a leather-pecker! He was delighted and he fixed everything they brought him.

And afterwards, Walter opened a fashionable hole-making boutique on one of the Big Tree's branches, and had customers from all over the forest. But he always punched the Duck sisters' leather belts without charge, because they had been responsible for getting him started in his new career.

The news that two Pandas were moving into an apartment in the Big Tree caused much excitement. After all, they were coming from China and nobody had ever met anyone from China before.

When they arrived, Pamela and Pat Panda turned out to be a lively young couple, very modern in their dress. Pat worked in TV and went to the studio in designer jeans and fancy shirts. Pamela worked in advertising and the young folk in the Big Tree were goggle-eyed at her short skirts and leotards. Sometimes she even wore an outrageous wig, of long, purple-dyed hair!

It wasn't long before others began to copy the Pandas' styles. The Hare brothers bought themselves expensive Jack Rabbit jeans, and the Ducklings were seen wearing leotards. Someone even said they had seen Louisa Lizard wearing a purple wig. She refused to wear it outside her own house because she had made it herself out of a pair of drapes!

Only the Pandas' downstairs neighbors, Connie and Charlie Cat, were unhappy about the newcomers. The Cats thought they made far too much noise. Evening after evening, the Cats were dozing quietly in front of their fire, when they were rudely awakened by loud music and the banging from the Pandas' apartment.

Eventually, after enduring the noise for a week, the Cats decided it was time to have a showdown with the Pandas.

"I'm going upstairs to complain," said Connie Cat. "We can't go on like this." She got up from her fireside chair and set off upstairs.

Charlie put down his cup of catmint tea and hurried after her. "Let's not be too hasty," he said.

When she reached the Pandas' door, Connie pressed the bell firmly, Charlie hovering behind her. The music was turned down and the door was opened by Pamela Panda.

"Come in," she said, beaming with delight. "Pat, the Cats have come to visit," she turned to her smiling husband.

Before the Cats could utter a word of protest, they were invited into the Pandas' apartment, made to sit in the best chairs, and being handed coffee and cookies. Connie had no time to complain. She was too busy talking to Pamela about color schemes, while Pat Panda and Charlie Cat exchanged opinions about the Big Tree's little league softball team.

It was only as the Cats were leaving, hours later, that Pamela asked the Cats why they had come up-stairs in the first place... "though we're so happy you did come."

Feeling rather ashamed, the Cats explained about the noise.

"We're so sorry," said the Pandas. "We didn't realize we were disturbing you. We'll be quieter in future, we promise."

And they were: the Pandas never again played music in their apartment loudly enough to disturb their best friends, the Cats.

The Little Worms Go Too Far

The Worms lived in a basement apartment in the Big Tree, next door to the Mouse family. Although they lived close together, the Mice tried to have as little as possible to do with the Worms, because the little Worms were terrible practical jokers, who seemed to get all their fun out of giving surprises and shocks to their neighbors.

For instance, there was the time when Mike Mouse was sliding down the banister on the Mouse staircase. Willy Worm had hidden himself alongside the railing, and when he popped his head up suddenly right in front of Mike, the young mouse got such a fright that he fell off completely and banged his nose so hard it began to bleed.

On another occasion, Wanda Worm hid amongst the plastic flowers which decorated the new hat that Mrs. Mouse had just bought. No sooner had she put the hat on her head than Wanda wriggled down over the brim and said: "Boo!" right into her face. The poor mouse nearly fainted.

The little Worms finally went too far with the trick that they played on Granny Mouse. They hid her favorite earthenware vase, and then Wally coiled himself up into the same shape and took its place. Granny Mouse was short-sighted so she

didn't notice the change. She took Wally to the tap and filled him up with water, then arranged flowers in him! It was only when she had placed

him on the table, that Wally suddenly uncoiled himself, shouting: "I fooled you!" Granny fell off her chair, the flowers flew everywhere, and water splashed all over the lovely, red rug on the floor.

Worst of all, the water made Granny's favorite book all wet. It was called *366 and More Cheesy Dreams*. It was full of tales of Mice Princes and Mice Princesses, and Mice Highwaymen, and Pirate Mice who buried their treasures in the holes that they had eaten in the cheese. When Granny saw her book looking like a damp diaper, she began to cry and that made things even wetter! She tried to wipe the water away with a towel, but only succeeded in rubbing some of the pictures away. She put it in front of the wood fire in the kitchen to dry off, but some sparks flew out and burned holes in some pages. She hung it up on the clothesline to dry in the air, but the wind blew some pages away. There was no doubt about it; her book would never be the same again.

So Granny Mouse went round to the Worms' house and complained to Mr. and Mrs. Worm about the behavior of their children. They apologized to her, of course, and said they would buy her a new copy of *366 and More Cheesy Dreams*. So Granny left, feeling a lot better: as long as she was getting to keep her favorite book.

When she had left, the Worms had a family

powwow. Wanda and Willy said they were very sorry that they had upset Granny Mouse so much and they promised they would not play tricks on their neighbors any more. But what could they do to make amends this time?

Then Wally had a bright idea. "Since Granny Mouse likes stories so much, why don't we put on a show just for her. We all love acting. We've got all the props. Let's write a play and stage it for Granny Mouse. That will make her very happy."

The whole Worm family, including their aunts and uncles and cousins, got to work. Mr. Worm wrote the script and Mrs. Worm made the costumes. Wally and Wanda had to play the leading

roles, of course, and some other worms were the villains, and the bit players. A stage was set up on the grass in front of the Big Tree.

And so, one evening the following week, Granny Mouse and her family were delighted to be invited to a Mouse Gala Evening at the theater. They sat entranced for hours, under the stars, watching the play which had been specially written for Granny, *The Mouse of Baghdad.*

At the end, everyone cheered and clapped, and Granny was presented with a new copy of her favorite book. And, after that, the Mice and the Worms were always the best of friends.

The Trouble With Planning a Vacation

Usually you cannot hear the Ants, but there are so many of them that whenever they have an argument in the family, all the Big Tree knows about it.

Mommy and Daddy Ant had been arguing for days about the family vacation. Mom, Annie Ant, wanted to go to the Termites' Rest Beach Hotel. Daddy, Adam Ant, wanted to go fishing with his friend, Walter Woodpecker. The little Ants wanted to go riding and canoeing in the mountains.

There was so much arguing going on that nervous, young Alvin Ant dropped and broke the big, painted leaf that was the family serving platter. Then little Alison Ant squeezed ketchup all over herself. The Ants' house was a mess.

Adam and Annie began to shout, then Adam went out to polish the family camper. This was something he always did at moments of stress.

Meanwhile, in the penthouse apartment, Cathy Crow and Walter Woodpecker were arguing about *their* vacation. Cathy wanted as usual to go to the Crow's Nest, a luxury, high-rise hotel overlooking the sea. Walter wanted to go fishing with his friend, Adam Ant.

Walter decided that there was no point in continuing to argue. He flew downstairs to talk to

Adam Ant, leaving Cathy still so angry that she threw a flower pot at Walter's picture by the window. The pot missed the picture, sailed out of the window and fell down... down... down... to land with a crash on the camper that Adam had just finished polishing. He was very upset!

Ants started rushing about in all directions. Walter put a wing round Adam to comfort him and Cathy flew down to apologize.

Fortunately, Cathy was a very wealthy bird, so she was able to pay for the Ants' camper to be made as good as new again. She also took all the Ants, and Walter, out to a splendid meal at the Dogs' Dinner Restaurant. And, during the meal, they decided to all go on vacation together, to the Fur and Feather Mountain Lodge, where the youngsters went riding and canoeing, Annie and Cathy sat beside the pool, and Adam and Walter went fishing after all!

Pat Panda Is Jealous

Pat Panda was a producer at the Woodland TV Studios. He loved his job, and he worked very hard. Sometimes, though, he worked too hard. For two weeks, he arrived home late every night because of rehearsals for a new TV show. His wife, Pamela, kept making him lovely dinners, but every night he would telephone and tell her that he would be late, so she ate them by herself.

One night, Pat came home very late indeed and found that Pamela had gone to bed and was asleep. He tiptoed into the bedroom and began to undress. Pat was just putting on his pyjamas when he heard Pamela say something in her sleep. He stood absolutely still, whiskers quivering. Pamela whispered: "Peter! What a lovely name! I'm so glad you're here even if Pat isn't!" Then Pamela turned over and was silent again.

Pat was stunned. "Peter? Who's Peter?" he puzzled anxiously. Was someone else coming round to have dinner with Pamela while he was working late?

"Oh dear!" thought Pat frantically. "It's my fault! I'm always late home. I wouldn't be surprised if someone else is keeping her company!"

All night long, poor Pat Panda tossed and turned in his bed, unable to sleep a wink. He promised himself that he would spend more time with Pamela from now on.

In the morning, Pat got up early for a change. He went down to the kitchen to make the coffee

and toast. When Pamela got up and found breakfast ready she was really pleased.

"How lovely of you to make breakfast – and especially today," she said.

Pat felt faint. "What do you mean?"

"I have a surprise for you. I waited up last night
to tell you but I fell asleep," eplained Pamela.

Pat felt worse.

"We're going to have a baby panda. I want to
call him Peter".

Pat Panda jumped for joy. He wasn't going to
lose Pamela, he was going to be a Papa Panda!

The Big Tree Sports Fans

Oliver Owl loved going to football games. Garry Goldfish, of course, was a water polo enthusiast. Although the two of them were the best of friends, they had never found a sport that they could both enjoy. They decided to change this and agreed that they would each give up their own favorite sport for one evening. Instead they would both go to watch the Woodland Tennis Tournament.

They bought tickets for the best center court seats and they ate lots of popcorn and drank lots of soda while they waited for the tournament to begin.

The first match was a mixed doubles, and then the trouble began! Every time a ball was hit into the netting, Garry thought a goal had been scored. Oliver got so angry at Garry jumping up and down on his tail and shouting "Goal" that he tried to disconnect the goldfish's water tank!

Then Garry got furious with Oliver for yelling "Touch down" whenever a player fell over. And when the players banged into each other as they were going for the ball, Oliver shouted "Obstruction" and waved his wings about so much that Garry slapped him with a fin.

Garry and Oliver caused such a rumpus that the tennis match had to be halted until they had both been thrown out. They were nearly sent to jail.

After that experience, Oliver went back to watching football games again and Garry returned to water polo. They stayed good friends by never going to any games together again!

Harry Horse did not actually live at the Big Tree. He lived in a big field called Prairie Pasture. It was over by the Big Tree railroad station. For the Ants or the Worms that was a long distance, but not for a big, strong horse like Harry, so he always thought of himself as a close neighbor... He knew everyone at the Big Tree and the folk there would welcome him for a visit whenever he trotted over, and sometimes they would come to see him in Prairie Pasture.

He had a fine, comfortable stable there which he had divided up into stalls. He used one stall as a dining-room, another for sleeping in, with thick straw on the floor and a large bucket of water in case he ever got thirsty during the night. There was a bathroom stall with a horseshoe-shaped window in the wall, and a kitchen stall with a set of the famous 'Nag' brand, brass cooking pots hanging from the rafters.

Everything about Harry's stable was well designed, because that's how Harry earned his oats, as a designer. He worked for Stallion Aviation, planning aircraft on his drawing board in the shapes of horses, and helicopters in the shapes of little ponies.

Harry had a great passion for potato chips and ate huge plates of them whenever he felt like a snack, between his regular feed bags of oats. He had just sat down in front of a plate of potato chips one day when he heard the sound of sobbing outside his stable door. He trotted out to see what was happening and found Bruce Bear sitting in the yard, crying his eyes out.

"What's the matter, Bruce?" asked Harry, sitting down beside the unhappy bear.

"They're going to change the Big Tree," sobbed Bruce. "It's going to be developed, and it'll all be concrete and plastic, and clean and tidy, and artificial..." Bruce couldn't go on, he was so upset.

"What are you talking about?"

So Bruce explained that there had been a Big Tree Residents' Association meeting the evening before. Everything had seemed normal. Fiona Fox said it was too hot in the Tree nowadays. Louisa Lizard said it was too cold. There were the usual complaints from the Ants, the Mice, and the Worms about their basement being damp in the

rainy season. Walter Woodpecker's roof leaked. It was just a normal Residents' Association meeting.

But then, up stood Jerry Jackal from the Woodland Real Estate Corporation.

"We want to buy this old ruin," he said. "Then we'll develop it and upgrade it. We'll give you all new, modern apartments. We'll get rid of all this old wood and earth and put in some nice fashionable concrete and plastic. The Big Tree will get a complete face lift."

The residents were silent. Many of them liked the Big Tree in its natural state. They weren't sure that they'd like it to be developed. Cathy Crow voiced her indignation: "I don't like the sound of it. Very unnatural!"

"You can't stand in the way of progress," said

Jerry Jackal. "Something must be done or the whole Tree will fall down."

The meeting had broken up in confusion. "And now," cried Bruce Bear, "what can we do?"

"What we have to do is renovate the Big Tree ourselves," said Harry Horse, neighing with determination. "I'll work out the designs!"

All the Big Tree residents started working with Harry's designs. Everyone helped. The Moles dug a new drainage system to stop the basement from getting damp. The Mice repaired the roof. The

Hares fixed the plumbing. Louisa Lizard gave the leaves a coat of new paint. Fiona Fox attended to odd jobs and the Owls made new rugs for the hallway floors.

In two weeks, the Big Tree was transformed. Jerry Jackal had to give up his plans to redevelop it. But he was invited, anyway, to the Good as New party to celebrate the Tree's new look. Harry was the guest of honor, and he was a very contented horse as he trotted home afterwards and looked back at the moon shining through the Big Tree's real leaves.

The Rescue of Oscar Owl

For days and nights, rain had been falling on the Big Tree. The leaves were soaked and streams of water were running down the branches and down the trunk.

The big rainwater tub at the top of the Big Tree, which supplied water to all the apartments, was completely full. Some big leaves had been blown into it by the wind and these were now blocking the overflow pipe. Suddenly water began to pour over the edge of the tub and down into the upper apartments.

It swept into the bedroom where the two young Owls lay sleeping. Olivia was the first to wake up. She lay without opening her eyes for a few dozy moments, wondering why her bed seemed to be rocking up and down. When she looked, she found that the room was flooded. She let out a hoot of alarm, just as little Oscar's bed began to float out of the window!

Ignoring her wet feathers, Olivia rushed to get her Mom and Pop. By the time they all returned, Oscar and his bed were outside the window, resting on the end of a long branch. None of the other Owls dared venture onto the branch, in case the bed might slide off and fall.

Everyone who lived in the Big Tree was now

awake. Some rushed out into the rain; others leaned out of their windows. They all had their hearts in their mouths when they looked up, or down, and saw Oscar's bed swaying back and forth in the wind. Any moment the branch might snap and down would come bed and Oscar!

Someone called the fire station and along came Captain Wolf and his brave team of firefighters. The branch creaked and sagged a little. Mrs. Owl fainted. Cathy Crow insisted that all the watching youngsters should go indoors immediately in case they saw something that would upset them. Captain Wolf ordered his team to hold out a large sheet of canvas under the branch. Then he began to climb the longest ladder. The wind tried to

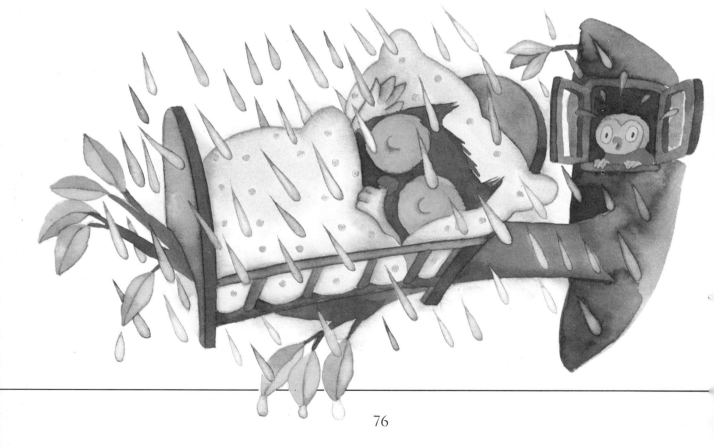

blow the ladder over, but little paws reached out to steady it. The wind tried to blow the canvas away, but the Big Tree folk rushed to help hold it in position. Finally, just as Captain Wolf grasped little Oscar in his arms and jumped down into the canvas sheet, everyone threw their woolens into it to make sure they had a soft landing.

"Hello, everyone," yawned Oscar, waking up. He sat up with Monty Mouse's sweater on his head, and said: "I dreamt that my bed went crazy and carried me into the shower!"

Sammy Centipede Gets the Boot

Willy Worm and Sammy Centipede looked at things from the same point of view. They went out everywhere together, until the day that Willy gave Sammy the boot!

It happened when Sammy went to the store to buy new shoes. Willy went with him. Sammy's mother gave him lots of money because it is expensive for a centipede to buy shoes – they have so many feet. Unfortunately, instead of just buying sensible shoes, Sammy felt the urge to express his colorful, inner self. He decided he would have a different style and a different color of shoes for each pair of feet. The whole store became involved. The assistants were not at all pleased. They had to bring out red shoes, green shoes, blue shoes, trainers, pumps, boots – Sammy wanted to see them all. He got carried away with the excitement and couldn't make a decision.

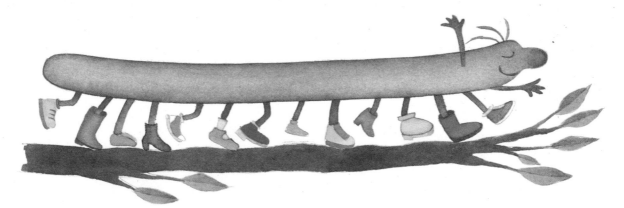

Willy decided to take some action or he would be spending the rest of his life in the shoe store! He borrowed a large boot from the manager, who was wishing Sammy had gone to another store to buy shoes. Then Willy and the shoe salesman stuffed Sammy into the boot and laced it so tightly he couldn't escape. Willy wrote the centipede's address on the sole and arranged for a mailman to take the boot away.

That evening, Sammy's family were amazed when he was delivered back inside a big boot. And after that, Willy never, ever, went shopping with Sammy again!

Arnold Ant's Bad Dreams

Arnold was a bright, young Ant – until he began to have bad dreams. He didn't have bad dreams just now and then. Arnold had bad dreams *every* night. As soon as he was tucked up in bed in his warm leaves and his mother had put out the light, Arnold would fall asleep and begin dreaming.

He dreamt about the strangest things. Arnold dreamt that Mommy Ant cried so much that his little sister was washed away by her tears. He dreamt that he was being chased by a big owl, which was really dumb because Mr. Owl had personally assured him that owls never chase ants. He dreamt that Aurora Ant, his favorite pop star, had lost her voice.

Every morning, Arnold was a very worried, little ant when he woke up. The first thing he had to do was to check to see if his bad dreams had come true. His family were confused by his questions.

"Alice," he asked his little sister, "did you have to swim far last night?"

"Mom, why does that owl keep chasing me?"

"Dad, do you think Aurora Ant will ever be able to sing again?"

Then Arnold would rush out of the kitchen, leaving his bewildered family behind, in order to watch TV for news of the lovely Aurora's health.

His mother and father were worried about him. They wondered if he was watching too much TV. They spoke to his teacher at school, and they all agreed that Arnold should talk with one of the school counselors. It was arranged for him to go

and see Freda Firefly, who was very experienced at helping agitated ants.

Arnold had always been reluctant to talk about his bad dreams. He was an independent, little ant and wanted to be able to fix things by himself, without help from anyone else. He was worried that his friends would think he was silly.

Freda Firefly, though, had a way with ants and it wasn't long before Arnold was telling her about his problems. She promised to help him.

"I think I know how to make your bad dreams go away," said Freda, flashing brightly.

And so, next evening, as soon as Arnold had fallen asleep, Freda appeared, hovering outside his bedroom window. Her warm glow drove away all the shadows, and cast a safe, comforting light over everything. And there she stayed, flashing

away all night long, and Arnold did not have a single bad dream. He woke up in the morning, happy and refreshed, and he didn't ask his family one wild question.

From then on, Mommy Ant took Freda Firefly's advice and put a cozy, night light beside Arnold's bed. He slept soundly every night, with never a bad dream to bother him.

Howie Hare had a crush on Louisa Lizard. Because he was very shy, like most hares, he never told Louisa about his feelings, and he was sure that she did not care for him at all.

Actually, Howie was wrong about this, because Louisa had a secret crush on him. Like most lizards, she was also shy, and, although she was a pretty, green thing, Louisa never dreamed that a fine, gray hare like Howie could like her.

It was such a big problem. When Louisa and Howie passed each other on the park paths, they would just smile at each other. Louisa would say to herself: "Howie is off to see a girl friend. He's got no time to talk to me."

Meanwhile, Howie would be thinking: "There goes lovely Louisa to meet a boy friend. I wish I was the lucky hare!"

At parties, Louisa talked to everyone except Howie, so that nobody would guess she had a crush on him. Howie was especially charming to everyone except Louisa, so that nobody would realize how he felt about her.

Of course, it was obvious to everyone at the Big Tree how they really felt about each other. Romantic folk would say to each other: "What a lovely couple Louisa Lizard and Howie Hare make! They are meant for each other!" But Louisa and Howie couldn't work that out for themselves.

One evening, a big party was held to celebrate the Foxs' wedding anniversary. All the Big Tree folk were there, singing and dancing and having fun. Of course, as usual, Louisa danced with all the guys except Howie and Howie danced with all the girls except Louisa.

Finally, Louisa could control her feelings no longer. She left the party in tears and went home to bed. When he found that Louisa had gone, the party no longer seemed to be any fun for Howie so he left as well. On his way downstairs, he came across a dainty, golden shoelace that had come off one of Louisa's dancing shoes. Trembling with emotion, Howie picked it up and held it close.

Louisa's shoe had come flying off on her way home, so she turned back to the party to try to find her golden shoelace. As she came to the foot of the stairs, there was Howie bounding about and clasping the shoelace to his heart.

As soon as the two bashful sweethearts saw each other, they threw caution to the winds, and themselves into each other's arms. It was their first embrace and all the Big Tree folk came out of the party to cheer and wish the happy couple lots of good luck.

Georgia the Ballerina

Georgia, the white goose, lived on the pond, not far from the Duckling sisters. Ever since she was a tiny gosling, Georgia loved the ballet. She had hoped that she might become a ballerina herself, but her teacher had convinced her that she didn't have the right figure for a dancer. But she was still a great fan and she went to every ballet that was performed by visiting companies at the Big Tree Playhouse.

Her favorite way to pass an evening was to settle down in front of the TV when the great star, Gooseyev, was dancing. Gooseyev was Georgia's dream dancer. She would have given all her tail feathers for a chance to dance Goose Lake with him. But she knew that could never be.

On her birthday, Daphne and Dinah Duckling prepared a wonderful surprise for Georgia. They knew that Walter Woodpecker had been a bit of a dancer himself when he was young. He was still very light on his feet. The Ducklings persuaded him, for Georgia's sake, to come out of retirement and limber up for a special gala performance.

The Playhouse was taken over for the event and the Ducklings bought a disc of the Goose Lake music. Then, in a dress and shoes specially made for the occasion, Georgia twirled onto the stage, to dance the famous *pas-de-deux*, with Walter trying very hard to substitute for Gooseyev. It was an unforgettable evening for everyone, especially for the ballet-loving little goose, Georgia.

Big Tree TVs Go Crazy

When there was a thunderstorm, the Big Tree was often struck by lightning. But it didn't seem to do it any harm – except for the time when lightning struck the TV antenna.

When the storm swept over the Tree, everyone was watching TV, because the popular quiz game, 'Trials of a Toad', was being shown. Big Tree hearts were beating fast as this week's contestant answered questions about toadstools.

The lightning hit the antenna with a crack and a sizzle and all the TVs went dark. Then the picture came back, but the 'Trials of a Toad' had vanished. Instead, there was a different picture on each set – and all from inside the Big Tree!

One TV showed the glass containing the old Goldfish's false teeth. Another had a picture of Wanda Worm painting onto her cheeks the beauty patches everyone had thought were natural. On another screen, Louisa Lizard was putting curlers onto her crest. Then there was a little paw reaching for the strawberry preserve. Some claimed it was Boris Bear, but he denied it because he only ate honey. So many secrets were revealed – the Big Tree was in turmoil.

Ben Bat, the TV repair man, came at once to fix everything right. It was only minutes before the game show was on the screen again, but it was days before everyone stopped talking about the night their TVs went crazy!

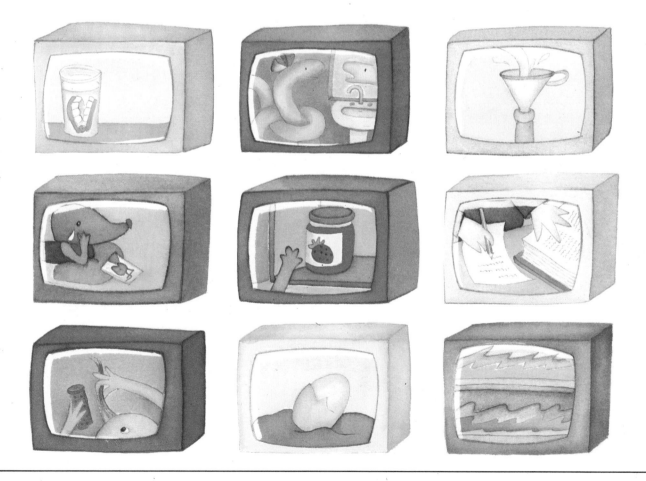

Goodbye, Granny Fox

Fiona Fox's grandmother was a very old vixen, whose fur had turned silvery-blue with age. Her real name was Fanny, but that had long been forgotten. She had been known as Granny Fox for as long as anyone could remember. She was the great-grandmother to just about all the cubs in the woods. If ever any one of them was unable to sleep, their mothers would send for Granny Fox, who would tell them stories and sing them songs until their eyes were closed.

Because she was so old, Granny Fox knew lots of things that had been forgotten by the younger ones. She knew how to make special carrot juice pick-me-ups for the Hare brothers. She knew how to make acorn compresses to put on Louisa Lizard's tail after it got caught in the door. And she could work lovely, traditional designs into the woolens she was always knitting for the children in the Ant family.

As Granny Fox grew older and less able to look after herself, she moved in with Fiona Fox. Fiona cared for her and gave her extracts of herbs to keep her strength up. But, although she grew weaker every day, Granny Fox was still as cheerful as she had always been.

One day, she said to Fiona: "I've never been to the movies. When I was young, there wasn't a movie theater at the Big Tree. Now I really would like to go once to the movies, before I die."

So Fiona wrapped Granny Fox up warmly in the shawl that the Owls had given her, and off they went, very slowly, to the movies. Granny thought it was all wonderful and returned home afterwards, very slowly again, an exhausted, but very happy old vixen.

That night, Granny Fox fell asleep as soon as her head touched her herb-filled pillow. She never woke again. In the morning, she was found lying there with a look of happy peace on her face. She was buried beside the old oak tree and everyone at the Big Tree brought flowers to say goodbye to Granny Fox, the Happiest Granny of the whole woods.

Kit Cat's Bad Moods

When Cousin Kit came to stay with the Cats at the Big Tree, he caused a real commotion in the hearts of all the girls. Kit was a young, handsome, gray cat, and he was a very sharp dresser, always wearing bright shirts and bow ties. There was no doubt that Kit was a very elegant and very eligible cat.

But no cat is perfect and Kit had his faults. He could be very moody at times, even hissing and spitting if you rubbed him the wrong way. He was better now at controlling these outbursts than he had been in the past, because he had gone to group meetings with other cats who had the same problem. But Kit's fur still stood on end if he thought he was being laughed at.

For instance, soon after his arrival at the Big

Tree, he heard a group of young Ants burst out laughing as he went past. They were playing their own games really, but Kit was convinced they were laughing at him, and he stormed past Alison Ant without speaking when she said "hello" to him later.

The same sort of thing happened on other occasions to one of the Mouse girls, and to a pretty Bear cub. They were both snubbed by Kit Cat.

Of course, such behavior soon made the young girls start to wonder if they really did want such a grumpy cat for a sweetheart after all?

Kit Cat finally learned his lesson when folk stopped inviting him to parties. He sat on the roof, feeling more and more lonely, while everyone else had fun. Then, one evening, Fiona Fox called up to him and asked Kit to come in and join them again. He was so happy at being asked back, that Kit Cat gave up his bad moods from then on, and had soon captured all the Big Tree hearts again.

The Wind-cycling Race

At the end of the semester, the children of the Big Tree School prepared a special surprise for their parents, relatives and friends. Instead of the usual stage show, with poetry recitals, music and songs, the children all took part in a wind-cycling race.

All dressed in their best clothes and looking proud of their youngsters, the audience sat down, ready to watch the race. Then the children lined up on their tricycles. Attached to each tricycle was a little mast and a big, bright sail. Sally Snipe, the first grade teacher, shouted, "Go" and Wally Woodchuck, the janitor, started the stopwatch.

The little paws and feet began pushing pedals as hard as they could, while the crowd cheered wildly. The wind blew into the colorful sails and the tricycles began to pick up speed. It was not a strong wind, but ants are not heavy, and it lifted Arnold and his tricycle right off the ground. He went flying in front of everyone else and was easily first across the line. Mike Mouse was next, his little nose bright red from his hard pedaling.

The judges awarded the wind-cycling race to Mike Mouse and he waved the big, gold cup about with joy. Arnold Ant was given an extra prize as the best hang-glider in the Big Tree School.

A Great Artist Comes for a Visit

The Worms had a famous relative, Woody Wood-worm, who was an artist who carved wood. His carvings were in all the best galleries. Woody lived like a gypsy, always moving around, never staying for long in one place. The Big Tree folk found out why, when he came to visit the Worms.

At first, Woody was a welcome guest. He lounged around, looking artistic, and all the Worms' neighbors found excuses to visit to have a look at the artistic genius. Once he had started work, though, nobody ever wanted to see Woody again.

As he only felt creative in the dark, he worked at night. He was very picky about the wood for his carvings and always cut it off the tree himself. The trouble was that Woody was a very quick worker and could chew through a branch in no time at all.

Every few minutes, throughout the night, down would crash another branch, and up would wake the Big Tree folk, who were lying in their beds trying to sleep. Woody became very unpopular.

After a week of Woody's creativity, everyone at the Big Tree looked dazed. They were so tired their eyes were glazed and they kept walking into things. They begged the Worms to ask Woody to leave, so the little genius departed to carve his works of art elsewhere. The Worms never once mentioned their famous relative to anyone at the Big Tree again.

As soon as school ended each afternoon, the Bear cubs, Boris, Basil and Betsy, did just as they'd been told, and hurried straight home. They didn't dawdle and they never spoke to strangers. Their friend, Oscar Owl, usually came with them. At the Bears' apartment, Mrs. Bear always had fruit juice and chocolate chip cookies waiting for them.

One afternoon, something terrible happened. Boris didn't come home. At first, Mrs. Bear didn't notice. The others came tumbling through the door, looking for their chocolate chip cookies.

"I'm starving," said Basil, trying to look thin. "Please may I have my cookie?"

"I could eat two," said Oscar, taking two.

"And three for me," said Betsy as she quickly put three cookies on her plate.

"How many for you, Boris?" asked Mrs. Bear. "That's odd. Where *is* Boris?"

Boris was nowhere to be seen. The others didn't remember seeing him on the way home, but they did remember him in the bushes just outside the school yard, looking for rocks for his collection.

An hour passed. Boris didn't come home. The Bears began to worry. They checked, but Boris was not with any of his friends. It was time for a search party. Taking a flashlight to light their path, chocolate chip cookies for energy, and lots of warm clothes, the Bears set off into the woods, accompanied by Walter Woodpecker, and Oliver Owl, who was the Big Tree's night watchman.

Of course, Boris was not in the woods. He was not even lost. He had spent hours in the bushes near the school yard, then wandered alongside the railroad tracks, still looking for rocks with unusual shapes. Then he decided to go home.

When he arrived home, the apartment was empty. That was strange. Boris was unhappy to find also that there were no chocolate chip cookies. He phoned Mona Mouse to complain.

Mona was very sympathetic. "Grown ups cause you nothing but worry," she said. "You just can't rely on them."

They decided to go out and search for the rest of Boris's family. They took a flashlight and a first aid kit in case of emergency. Off they went into the woods.

A flashlight flashed through the trees. It was the Bears' party. Boris and Mona had found them!

There were some red faces that night at the Big Tree when everything was explained. Boris promised that, in future, he would always come straight home from school. Mrs. Bear promised that, no matter what happened, she would save Boris his share of cookies!

A Good Day's Work for the Movers

Cathy Crow and Walter Woodpecker had been engaged for a long time. Big Tree folks were just beginning to wonder if they ever would get married, when the wedding date was set.

The happy couple started planning their home. They decided to keep both their apartments. They would rent Cathy's and live in Walter's. But first, it had to be refurnished.

They sent for Pablo Parrot, the fashionable interior designer. He looked at Walter's furniture, sniffed in disdain, and said: "Everything's got to go, darlings! Away with those chairs. You need big cushions to sit on. Out with those lamps. Spotlights, they're the rage now. And that table is just firewood. You don't need a table. Most people dine at restaurants!"

Cathy and Walter did as they were told. Out went all Walter's old furniture, and they bought new furniture from a delighted furniture salesman.

Then the Ants were hired to move the furniture. Perhaps because ants can carry such heavy weights, the Ant Agency always got the job of moving furniture in and out of the Big Tree. All the Ants worked in the company: grandparents, parents, children, aunts, uncles and cousins. At work, they all wore blue overalls, with a red label on the back, and the letter 'T', meaning Transportation, on it.

As an old friend, Adam Ant promised Walter a discount. The contract was signed and dozens of ants carried all the new furniture into Walter's apartment.

Then Cathy changed her mind! Walter's place was too cluttered. The furniture had to go to her apartment instead.

The Ants put their overalls back on and everything was carried out of Walter's apartment and into Cathy's.

Then Walter changed *his* mind! He had to assert himself. He couldn't allow Cathy to change all their arrangements. The furniture must go where they had agreed in the first place – back in his apartment!

Once again the Ants moved everything. They had just finished placing it all in Walter's apartment when Cathy decided that she was making a big mistake. She was too young to marry just yet. She would remain engaged to Walter for now, and perhaps get married next year.

Luckily, the Ants hadn't bothered to take their overalls off. They carried the furniture back to the store, where the disappointed salesman put it all out in the showroom again. Then, they got a really big paycheck from Walter, and went off and bought themselves a new trailer for vacations.

Otis Otter and the Red Spots

Otis Otter's mother came from the south and she had lovely, golden brown fur. His father was born on an island in the east and he had dark, almond shaped eyes. Otis Otter had golden brown fur, like his mother, and almond-shaped eyes, like his father. He was so handsome that he made all the girls at the Big Tree school dreamy-eyed.

The other boys wanted to be just like him. If Otis wore a blue tie, then they all had to wear blue ties. If Otis started wearing suspenders instead of a belt, off came all their belts.

This was all very fine until the day Otis came home from playing by the stream with a face covered in red spots.

"Chickenpox, said his mother. She called for his father.

"Chickenpox", said Otis' father. He sent for the doctor.

"Chickenpox", said Dr. Mole. "Straight to bed, my young otter."

When the other children heard that Otis had chickenpox, they decided immediately that they had to have it too. Suddenly, the Big Tree had a chickenpox epidemic. All the young faces were covered in red spots – except for Wilfred Worm. He tried and tried so hard, but worms can't catch chickenpox, so he had to paint his spots on!

The Alphabet Monster Makes a Visit

All the young, neighborhood animals went to the Big Tree School. They left home at the same time every morning, each one with a schoolbag. They met on the way to school to become a noisy, chattering stream of mischief.

In the school yard, they ran around and played tricks on each other. The teachers, Sally and Sandra Snipe, had to work very hard to get them to stand in line and behave themselves, before allowing them into the classrooms.

Sally would shout: "Oscar Owl, behave yourself!" And Sandra would call out: "Boris Bear, stop that!" Then both together would yell at Mike Mouse, who could never hear anything, because he always wore earphones and listened to rock music on his portable radio.

Once in the classrooms, there was more noise and confusion. Chairs were banged about, books thumped onto desks, and a few, final scuffles took place. But, one morning, an unnatural silence fell upon the class. An enormous shadow had appeared on the window which led on to the corridor. It was like a head, with one fierce eye, but it was a monster's head, of a shape that none of the youngsters had ever seen before.

The entire class trembled, squeaked with fright, and thought longingly of their mothers.

"Miss Snipe! Help! It's a monster!" they yelled.

Miss Snipe heard their cries and hurried into

the classroom. She saw at once what the 'monster' was. Outside, Wally Woodchuck, the janitor, was working by lamplight at a table. The monster's shadow was only the shadow of his undone shirt cuff, and the 'eye' was the buttonhole!

Sally Snipe thought quickly: "How can I make this help the children?" Then she had an idea. "Don't be afraid", she said. "It's only the silly, old Alphabet Monster. He can't hurt you if you know your letters."

Then she began to ask the youngsters questions about their homework. They had been asked to learn their ABCs. It was really remarkable, but they all gave her the correct answers, until, suddenly, the monster's head disappeared from the window, to be replaced by the shadow of a fairground carousel.

"It must be playtime", cried Mike Mouse. The youngsters squealed with excitement and rushed to the door. As they poured out into the corridor, they found that Wally Woodchuck was peeling an orange. The shadow of the peel going round was the 'carousel' they had seen.

As Miss Snipe watched them go, she couldn't help thinking she'd have a more orderly class, if only she had a monster at the window every day!

The Mystery of the Missing Ruby

Big Tree folks are always happy to tell the story of Tommy Toad's missing ruby. The chief of detectives, Inspector Barry Badger, will also try to impress you with his account of how he solved the case, but there are those who believe that the credit should really go to young Betsy Bear.

The mystery began one morning in Tommy Toad's workshop. Tommy was the Big Tree's watchmaker and jeweler. Before he began work each day, he always went round all the clocks and

watches in the store, checking that they were telling the correct time. Then he put his stock of jewels out on display. There were diamonds that twinkled like stars, emeralds that looked like cats' eyes, blue sapphires, white pearls, and, in pride of place, there was the big ruby that gleamed like a bonfire on a cold winter's night. Except that, on this particular morning, there was no ruby. It had disappeared.

Tommy searched for it everywhere, without success, then he sent for the great detective, Barry Badger. He came at once, with his faithful police dogs. He wore his great detective's outfit, with a white, belted raincoat and a hat pulled down over his eyes.

Barry Badger carefully examined the scene of the crime. He found three clues. There was a piece of blue cloth caught on a rosebush outside the back window. Beside it, there lay a round piece of glass. Inside the workshop, there was some white powder on the corner of the empty display case.

One by one, the Big Tree residents were questioned. Most of them had watertight alibis. But the finger of suspicion began to point towards Cathy Crow!

First of all, Babs Bear said that the piece of blue cloth looked very like a part of Cathy's cloak. Then, Dr. Mole expressed his opinion that the

piece of glass *might* be from a pair of glasses of the kind used by Cathy. Finally, Louisa Lizard was sure that the white powder was the same as that used by Cathy Crow for dusting her underwing feathers.

Inspector Badger decided to take the crow in for questioning. Everyone watched with dismay as she was taken away by the police dog, her wings cuffed in front of her, all the while protesting: "This is a big mistake! I am innocent!"

Nobody was more appalled than her beloved Walter Woodpecker. He vowed he would prove her innocence. He went back to Cathy's apartment for her glasses, found them and took them round to show Dr. Mole that there was no glass missing from them.

But Dr. Mole had been called out to attend to

Betsy Bear, who had a cherry stone stuck between her teeth. Dr. Mole was really an optician, not a doctor of medicine, nor a dentist, but because he lived in the Big Tree, the residents there consulted him no matter what was wrong with them!

Dr. Mole arrived at the Bears' apartment to find Betsy wailing like a siren. She had been eating a dish of cherries when a stone had become lodged in her tooth. Quickly, Dr. Mole got out a pair of pliers, told the young bear to open her mouth, and then gently extracted the stone. He put it on the table. And then everyone realized that it was not a cherry stone at all. It was a ruby, as red as a bonfire on a cold winter's night. It was Tommy Toad's missing ruby.

Inspector Badger was sent for at once. He questioned Betsy and she told him how she came to be

eating a ruby! She had been out in the woods the previous evening when Wes Weasel had rushed past her. He was wearing a blue cloak at the time, and had a sack of flour over his shoulder. As he passed her, a cherry had fallen from his pocket, and Betsy had heard him complaining about losing the glass from his watchface.

Trying to be helpful, Betsy picked the cherry up, and called after Wes: "If your watch is broken, take it to Tommy Toad..." She had been going to go on and say: "You've dropped a cherry", but at the mention of Tommy Toad's name, Wes had shouted at her: "Hush! Hush! Not a word!" and run away. Betsy had taken the cherry home and put it in the cherry dish in the kitchen. And then, today, she'd eaten it!

Of course, Cathy Crow was released immediately and escorted home by Inspector Badger.

Wes Weasel was taken into custody, and at the precinct house he confessed to stealing Tommy's ruby, *and* a bag of flour from the Bears' kitchen. He was put on probation and he promised not to steal anything ever again.

Betsy Bear received a 'detective' badge from Inspector Badger which she put on her wall, and a box of cakes, which she ate immediately.

The Great Teacup Disaster

Louisa Lizard was visiting Babs Bear. They were having a lovely chat and sipping mint tea when the great disaster happened. Babs knocked her teacup over. Mint tea went all over Louisa's elegant dress. Louisa jumped up quickly – the tea was hot – and dropped *her* cup, which broke into pieces on the floor.

Well, you might think that that's not such a great disaster, but wait, there's more!

Cathy Crow passed by the Bears' apartment as all this was happening. She heard the raised voices

and the noise of a breaking cup. She heard enough!

Cathy rushed at once to Walter Woodpecker. "Babs Bear and Louisa Lizard are having an argument and throwing cups at each other!"

Walter thought his fishing partner, Adam Ant, ought to be told. He phoned him with the news. "Babs and Louisa are having a terrible fight, They're covered in bruises!"

When she heard this, Annie Ant decided to ask Oliver Owl to act as peacemaker. After all, Oliver *was* the night watchman, and someone had to stop Babs and Louisa from smashing up all the furniture and wrecking the house.

Other Big Tree folk heard the news. Within an hour of the cup breaking, a committee had been

set up in order to get money to buy dishes and new furniture for the Bears' devasted apartment, and to pay the hospital expenses for Babs and Louisa.

The committee was just bringing food and blankets to the two victims, when they stepped outside the Bears' front door and kissed each other good-bye. They were both well, and the Bears' apartment turned out to be undamaged.

The committee quickly held another meeting and agreed to organize a party for everyone at the Big Tree to celebrate a happy ending to the great teacup disaster. They all learned it is better to know the facts before a story is repeated to other residents of the Big Tree.

The Fireflies Take a Vacation

The Fireflies lived in a tall bush near the Big Tree. Fred worked for the Highways Department. It was his job to make sure the traffic signals worked properly. If a signal stopped working, Fred Firefly would go inside and take over until it could be repaired. He had special sweaters that he wore when he was on the job, red, green and orange, depending on which light was not working.

Freda was a counselor at the Big Tree School, where she helped young ants to cope with bad dreams. She did lots of other helpful work. If someone forgot to buy candles for a birthday cake, Freda would call out a group of fireflies, called Partysavers, and they would all twinkle on the bare cake. For the Big Tree Soccer Club, Freda was the official floodlighter because they couldn't

afford real lights. She also announced goals, in
flashes: a long flash for a bears' goal, and a short
flash for an owls' goal.

Freda and Fred hadn't had a vacation for years.
Freda decided to go to the beach for two weeks.

Fred said his work was too important and waved
goodbye to her at the railroad station. After two
days, he missed her so much that he took a train
and joined her.

The Big Tree was a big mess without the Fireflies. There were no candles at all on Oscar Owl's birthday cake. The soccer club couldn't play any games. The traffic signals stopped working completely and Annabel Ant on her tricycle ran into Dr. Mole at a dark intersection. Everything was awful!

In fact, Freda and Fred Firefly were so important to life at the Big Tree that after they had been away for one week, everyone else stopped work and took a week's vacation also. They just couldn't manage without their very own Fireflies.

The Big Tree's Flying Saucer

It seemed like a normal night at the Big Tree.

At about eleven o'clock, the night watchman, Oliver Owl, was awake as usual, reading through his favorite joke book, *Owls of Laughter*, by the light of his office lamp.

Constance Cat was lying in her bed, unable to sleep. She got up at about eleven o'clock to get some fresh air and was very angry to find the bedroom window handle had fallen off. She tried to

wake her tomcat, Clarence, but he just twitched his ears, nose and whiskers and carried on sleeping soundly.

Matilda Mole's aunt, Molly, sat down before her mirror to brush her fur before going to bed at about eleven o'clock. She noticed that there was a cobweb hanging in front of the mirror, then she realized that the mirror itself was cracked.

"What bad luck", Molly said angrily and she went to bed without brushing her fur at all.

At about eleven o'clock, Walter Woodpecker and Adam Ant were having their last card game of the night. Suddenly they both discovered that the cards had been changed. Neither of them was holding any cards except threes. They threw down their hands, accused each other of cheating, and stormed off to their beds without wishing each other goodnight.

Five Big Tree folk were awake at about eleven o'clock. There was Constance Cat who couldn't sleep. There was Molly Mole who was worrying

about bad luck. There were Walter Woodpecker and Adam Ant who were each fretting because their best friend had cheated at cards. And there was Oliver Owl, who never slept at night anyway, because he was the night watchman.

Suddenly, there was strange, flickering light in the dark sky above the Big Tree. All five of them saw it quite clearly. It looked like a glowing saucer, covered in fireflies, but it was a flying

saucer and it buzzed away like a hive full of bees. Constance Cat thought grumpily that the janitor

had put up a faulty lamp outside her apartment. She leaned out of the window, stuck out her tongue, and cried: "Oh, stop it now. You're annoying me!"

A yellow ball of light flashed out of the saucer, whizzed across the night sky and struck Constance's whiskers, turning them bright silver.

When Molly Mole saw the light she thought that at last her friend, Morgan Mole, had come to ask her to elope with him. She waved and blew a kiss out of the the window. The saucer replied

with another yellow ball of light which whizzed into Molly's room and put a bright, silver streak on
her fur.

In his room, Walter thought that the light must

be a signal from Adam Ant, who wanted to come
over and say he was sorry for cheating at cards.
Adam Ant thought the light was a signal from
Walter. Both of them got out their flashlights and
flashed a signal in reply out of their windows. Two
yellow balls of light flashed out of the saucer. Both

Walter and Adam found a bright, silver playing card, three of diamonds, on their tables.

Because he was the night watchman, Oliver Owl made no mistake about the light in the sky. He knew exactly what it was. He hurried to the phone and rang every apartment in the Big Tree.

"Wake up!" said Oliver. "Get dressed quickly and come outside. A flying saucer has come to visit the Big Tree!"

In no time at all, dozens of sleepy, rumpled animals were standing outside looking at the flying

saucer, which was still buzzing away like a bee-hive. They rubbed their eyes, looked again, pinched each other to make sure they really were awake, and then stared in silent wonder at the glowing object above them.

It's impossible to discover what really happened that night at the Big Tree after that. Some say that the saucer flew away and everyone went quietly back to bed. Others insist that the flying saucer actually landed and took all the Big Tree folk on board for a short trip around the moon. Then they were brought back to the Tree and made to promise, cross their hearts, never, never to tell anyone about it.

It's certainly true that after that night the youngsters at the Big Tree School took a great interest in stars and planets and space travel.

And, of course, if we go to the Big Tree we can see for ourselves Constance Cat's silver whiskers, the silver streak in Molly Mole's fur, and the silver three of diamonds playing cards in Walter Woodpecker's and Adam Ant's apartments.

Peter Panda is Born

Early one morning when it was still dark, some of the Big Tree residents were awakened by the sounds from the Pandas' apartment. Doors were opened and shut, Pamela and Pat Panda were calling out to each other, and then there was the noise of the Pandas' car being moved out of the garage.

It was easy to guess what was happening. Pamela Panda was about to give birth to her cub. She had been waiting for a long time for this moment, and so had everyone else at the Big Tree.

When her bag was packed, Pat drove Pamela very carefully to the Super Sapling Clinic, where all the Big Tree babies were born.

Behind them, they left the Tree buzzing with excitement. Everyone was up and dressed, because when a baby is born, everyone wants to share in the joy of the moment. Maggie Mole prepared a large supply of her special, celebration, barley drink. Fiona Fox gathered all the youngsters together and told them stories about other Big Tree babies. As quietly as only little mice can, the Mouse family slipped into the Pandas' apartment to leave toys in the nursery that had been prepared for the new cub. Babs Bear sat down to finish embroidering the initials 'PP' on the cradle cover she had been making. She knew the little Panda was going to be called Peter, because Pamela had dreamed all about it weeks ago.

Dr. Mole was constantly on the phone to the clinic, and kept everyone up to date with the news. He shouted for silence so that he could hear what the nurse was saying to him.

"Wonderful news", he told the Big Tree folk.
"Peter Panda has arrived safely!"

There was much cheering and clapping. Louisa
Lizard, as always at such moments, burst into
tears. Walter Woodpecker got so emotional he
kissed the bird standing next to him, which happened to be one of the Duckling sisters. Cathy
Crow saw him doing it and glared at him.

Suddenly the phone rang again. It was the clinic. Pamela had had another cub; Peter Panda had
a sister. Twins were a double joy.

Then the phone rang again. Pamela had had

two more cubs, one male, one female. She was the mother of quadruplets four baby pandas!

Everyone began to prepare. Louisa's favorite wicker basket and two drawers from Cathy's antique dresser were brought in as extra beds. More sheets were produced from store rooms, and three more feeding bottles.

Finally, only the names were missing! What should the other cubs be called. There were long discussions about this, even arguments sometimes, before it was agreed to propose Paul, Penny, and Polly to the Panda parents. And they were delighted with the choice and so the cubs were named.

Wes Weasel, the Master Burglar

Wes Weasel was the Big Tree's very own burglar. Everyone knew him. Whenever they couldn't find something they were looking for, Big Tree folk would nod wisely to each other and say, "Wes must have taken it." Actually, Wes probably had not taken it at all; they had just mislaid it themselves. But it was easier to blame Wes, and Wes was very proud of his reputation as a master burglar. He dressed up in all the latest burglar's gear, which he had ordered from a mail order catalog. He had a mask and a big sack for loot and, best of all, he had a set of skeleton keys that would open all the Big Tree doors.

Unfortunately, on his first night out with the keys, Wes lost them somewhere inside the Mouse home. He looked everywhere, but he had to leave without them. He was very sad.

Mrs. Mouse was not happy either next day when she found the missing skeleton keys – inside her soup pot! And the Mouse youngsters complained loudly about the odd, metallic taste of their mother's pea soup.

The police took the keys to Wes Weasel's house to ask if they were his, and Wes was so pleased to see them again that he said: "Yes." So the police locked him up and he spent a week in jail.

The Goldfish Family Portrait

A nice family photograph, that's all the Goldfish wanted; one that they could copy and send to relatives and friends.

Naturally, there were problems! Nobody at the Big Tree had any experience of underwater photography. Harry Horse took a few test pictures in the stream, but couldn't get a fish in any of them, only weeds. No one else had any better luck.

So the Goldfish gave up the idea of having the picture taken underwater. They put on their face masks, strapped water tanks on their backs, and came on land. Then they stood in a group under trees, while different Big Tree residents used their cameras. The photos were fine, but you couldn't tell one Goldfish from another with masks on!

Instead of a family photo, they asked Sandy to

paint a family portrait. Day after day, he dived into the stream, making sketches with an underwater pen. Back in the studio, he began to paint.

The portrait turned out to be a remarkable work of art. The Goldfish were delighted, but they never got to keep the picture. Peregrine Pig, the Tree's art critic, fell in love with the painting when he saw it, and insisted that it should be put on display at the Woodland Art Museum.

And that's where the Goldfish have to go, wearing their face masks and water tanks, if they want to see their family portrait!

A Very Special Birthday

There was a particular reason why all the youngsters hurried home that afternoon from school and
nursery. They didn't dawdle as they usually did.
They didn't splash in puddles or play games with
each other. They all ran straight home. And, after
work, their mothers and fathers did just the same.
There was no stopping to chat about the Woodland Tennis Championships or the latest forest
fashions. Everyone, young and old, was rushing
home to prepare for a very special birthday.

It was going to be a spectacular party. It was going to be an extraordinary party for an extraordinary birthday. The festivities were not for any of
the animals who lived at the Big Tree, not even for
one of the Ants, and there were so many of them
that they had birthday parties nearly every week!
What was going to be celebrated that evening was
nothing less than the birthday of the Big Tree it-

self. Trees only celebrate a birthday every hundred years, so tonight was the Tree's tenth birthday party. It was a thousand years old. It was the most beautiful, the tallest, *and* the oldest tree in the woods.

Over the centuries, the Tree had been greatly loved by many animals. Even some famous people had been to its birthday parties or sent presents. The first president of the land where the Big Tree lived had even sent one of his soldiers to the Tree with a greetings card and a gift of a large pocket watch. As the Big Tree didn't have any pockets, the watch was put instead on one of its branches.

It still hung there, though the wind had long ago blown the hands off.

The Big Tree was loved by everyone in the way that they loved their old grandparents. They thought the Tree was mysterious and clever and brave, and had lived through many exciting times.

On this particular evening, the old Tree was resting quietly. It had passed the day dozing in the sunshine, and was now gently rustling in the wind, watching clouds pass slowly across the face of the moon. The Tree suddenly realized it was all alone. There was no one home in it, not even Oliver Owl, the night watchman. How strange! There was no Mouse family watching TV, there was no Clarence Cat in his bed nursing his sore whiskers, there were no Hares playing with their computer. Where *was* everybody?

Then, deep in the woods, something stirred. It wasn't the breeze, it was Harry Horse, who clopped out of a thicket of brambles, pulling a wagon behind him. Piled high on the wagon was a big, fancy box and bottle after bottle of Maggie

Mole's celebration barley drink. After the wagon came all the Big Tree residents, each carrying a cup or a glass. They had come to drink a toast to the Tree, crying out: "Happy Birthday, Big Tree!"

Everyone cheered, then the big, fancy box was lifted out of the wagon and put down in front of the Tree. Eager paws fastened to the box the big, colorful Mr. Marvel balloon left behind by Ossie Ostrich. The little paws let go when someone shouted: "Now," and the balloon rose in the air. It lifted the box to the top of the Tree, where the box opened and a shower of sparkling fireworks exploded.

After that wonderful start to the birthday party, there were cakes to eat, more fireworks, barley drinks for everyone, and then more fireworks. Everyone poured a glass of barley drink over the Tree's roots so that it could also enjoy the party spirit. The youngsters from the school sang a song specially written for the occasion by their teachers, the Snipe sisters. Tommy Toad croaked a speech of congratulations on behalf of all the Big Tree's residents, then Louisa Lizard ran along each branch hanging bunches of flowers everywhere.

Finally, everyone joined hands to hug the Big Tree right round its trunk. It wasn't easy to do, but you have to make a special effort for a thousand-year-old friend!

Monty Mouse, who lived in the Big Tree, was the best clothes designer and tailor in the woods. Actually, he was the only one in the woods, but everyone knew he was the best, and animals traveled from far and wide just so that they could have a garment designed and made by Monty.

Because he was a designer himself, Monty had always dreamed of going to a fashion show sometime, especially in Paris, the famous city where the best designers worked. Unfortunately, he did not know how to get to Paris. Also, he had been advised that it was most unlikely that a mouse without an invitation would be allowed into a show.

When his wife suggested that he should hold his own fashion show, Monty was very excited. Preparations were soon, under way, and for weeks before the event, everyone talked of nothing else. A big banner was stretched right across Woodland

Way, proclaiming: 'Grand Fashion Show – The Creations of Monty Mouse.' He asked some of his Big Tree friends to be models. They spent time learning how to walk strangely.

The show took place in front of the Big Tree. Model after model was greeted with loud applause. The only sour note was the way in which the ruder young animals whistled when Cathy Crow hopped out in her swimsuit. The loudest cheers were reserved for a pair of Monty's famous suspenders.

After that evening, Big Tree residents boasted that it was Monty Mouse who set the fashions really: in Paris just copied him!

Frances Frog, the Quiz Queen

Frances was a cheerful, hard-working frog. She delivered the mail to the Big Tree neighborhood. In every kind of weather, Frances could be seen on her red bicycle, going from door to door, handing out postcards, letters and packages.

One day, Frances delivered a letter to herself! It was from her favorite TV quiz show, telling her that she had been chosen to participate in next week's phone-in competition. The prize was a small fortune in lily leaves, and a free cruise on 'The Quagmire Queen' – the famous ship.

Frances was very excited on the evening of the show. She loved the host, Squiffy Squirrel. She thought he was so handsome, so clever, so funny. She watched the studio contestants trying to answer questions on flowers, and cooking, and atomic energy, and she grew more and more nervous. When the phone rang, she almost fainted.

Squiffy asked Frances to name all the famous people on the postage stamps that were being shown on the TV screen. Frances could hardly believe her luck! All day long, every day, she was looking at these stamps on the letters she had to deliver. She knew every name. She had won the competition.

Everyone in the Big Tree watched the next Squiffy Squirrel Show, to see Frances being presented with her prizes-lily leaves, a ticket for the boat cruise, and a kiss from Squiffy Squirrel. It was the greatest moment in the frog's life!

How Harry Horse's Dream Came True

Harry Horse was very popular with all the Big Tree residents. He was a big friendly steed, who was always pleased to give a helping hoof to someone if they needed it. He gave rides to all his friends, and could often be seen trotting around Prairie Pasture with someone on his back – Bruce Bear, or Georgia Goose, or Sandy Squirrel, or even the entire Ant family, all at the same time.

Harry thought that everyone ought to have the chance of going horseriding at some time in their lives. He felt strongly about this because, ever since he had been a colt himself, he had longed to ride a horse. But, of course, he hadn't even had a rocking horse when he was young. Nobody gives a horse a rocking horse! All the other Big Tree kids had rocking horses in their nurseries – even the little Ants, though you needed a magnifying glass to find theirs. Only Harry Horse at the Big Tree had never had a chance to sit on any kind of horse's back.

Harry's friends decided to do something about this. Sandy Squirrel drew a picture of a horse. Working from this, Willy Woodworm modeled a wooden horse. Monty Mouse made a soft, velvet covering for the wooden horse, and Tommy Toad took two emeralds out of the display case for the

eyes. Finally, using their computer skills, the Hare brothers designed and fitted an engine inside the horse, so that it could move.

The completed wooden horse had red ribbons tied to its mane and tail and then it was led to Harry's stable. Bruce Bear made a little speech on behalf of Harry's friends and then they presented the horse to him.

His joy and delight brought tears to everyone's eyes. Then they watched as Harry fulfilled his childhood dream, and went for a gallop around Prairie Pasture on his very own wooden horse.

Warren Wolf, the Kind-hearted Criminal

Captain Wolf was the brave chief of the Big Tree firefighters. He wore a splendid uniform, specially made by Monty Mouse, the famous designer. Looking at this imposing animal, nobody would have guessed that he had an embarrassing secret. He had a criminal cousin called Warren Wolf.

Warren had been led astray by stories of the exploits of Wes Weasel, the Big Tree's master burglar. Warren decided at an early age that he too wanted to have a police record. Why should Wes be the only one in the neighborhood with a bad reputation?

One dark, starry night, Warren set out for some mischief. He had dressed for the occasion in his best dark clothes, and he wore a mean mask to hide his identity. Only his brush was still visible.

He headed for Wally Woodchuck's apartment.

Warren had heard it rumored that Wally stayed out late every night, playing tiddly-winks with Georgia Goose. It was a perfect set up. Warren could sneak in and steal everything!

Warren found that Wally had even left a bedroom window open for him. In a flash he slipped in, turned on his flashlight – and nearly collapsed with fright! Wally wasn't out playing tiddly-winks at all. He was lying fast asleep in bed.

It was obvious that the poor, little woodchuck had a fever. His nose and ears were pink. His breathing was noisy. Beside the bed was an empty cup, and there were books and liniment on a table.

The sight of the poor, little woodchuck lying there, ill and alone, moved Warren's kind heart. He couldn't steal from a sick animal.

Instead, he pretended that he was the district nurse! He gave Wally a hot barley drink, rubbed his chest with liniment, then read him a story from one of the books, before tucking in the grateful woodchuck and saying goodnight.

Then Warren climbed out of the window and ran home as fast as he could before anyone saw him doing a good deed!

A Movie Director Visits the Big Tree

Warren Wolf's brother, William, had left the Big Tree some years ago, gone to Hollywood, and become a famous movie director. Few would ever forget his award-winning series of dog movies, featuring Laddie, the almost wolf-like star.

One fine day, William Wolf returned to the Big Tree. He was scouting for locations for his next big-budget epic, *The Flea*, which would feature all sorts of special effects. He set up his director's chair beside Woodland River and looked around him. Since he didn't want anyone to know that he was a movie wolf, he disguised himself in a striped shirt and dark glasses.

The disguise didn't work. Perhaps it was the director's chair or perhaps Warren Wolf said something, but news soon got around that there was a famous movie director sitting by the river. Big

Tree folks with dreams of stardom went to see him.

Olga Owl, who wanted to be a singer, insisted on hooting in front of him. The Worms, who had a great interest in the theater, came in a group to perform a few plays. Cathy Crow, who wrote poems, recited some of her best verses to William.

After a day of this, the great movie director abandoned all hope of using the Big Tree as a location. William folded his director's chair under his arm, put away his scripts, and, still wearing his dark glasses, crept quietly away in the dusk.

The Big Tree Sports Meet

From the moment it was decided to hold a Big Tree Sports Meet residents could think of little else. Those who weren't in training for the various events were involved in painting white lines, sewing finishing tapes, and digging sandpits.

The whole neighborhood was buzzing. At any time of the day, and sometimes the night, you might see mice and moles running time trials. The timekeeper, of course, was always Tommy Toad. You had to beware of ants lifting weights, or of groups of worms playing volley-ball. Unless you were careful, you could be jumped on by hares or frogs. Everywhere there were animals in track-suits, running, hurdling, jumping, or just lying down, puffing and exhausted.

Competitors were coming from near and far. A team of deer had put their names down for the high hurdles. A number of crocodiles, all belly flop specialists, had already arrived and could be seen lounging in the mud around the pond. The Duckling sisters had given up swimming there until the sports meet was over! On the volley court, some giraffes were practicing, flicking the ball to each other with their heads. The local standing jump experts, the hares and frogs, were watching, in dismay, a kangaroo doing warm-up exercises.

When the sports meet finally began, there was an unfortunate incident in the very first event. In the free-style wrestling, Mike Mole got angry because Erik Eagle, his opponent, pecked him when

Captain Wolf, the referee, wasn't looking. Captain Wolf warned Mike for biting. Mike complained that it was not fair if the referee could see bites but not pecks. That upset Captain Wolf and he awarded the bout to Erik!

A new Big Tree record was set by Phineas Pheasant in the spiral jump. When the starting pistol was fired, Phineas clucked and took off in a magnificent corkscrew, which easily outdistanced all the other contestants. Later, Phineas became so excited that he made a spiral jump when *any* starting pistol was fired!

Walter Woodpecker became the hero of the Big Tree with his unexpected victory in the backward running race. When he was asked afterwards to what he attributed his success, he said it was due to the practice that he'd had, running backwards to escape from the objects thrown at him during lovers' quarrels with his fiancée, Cathy Crow.

The big track event of the meeting was the

radish relay. The hares' team failed to finish because one of the runners ate their radish and arrived at the handover point with nothing to pass on to the next hare except a burp. There were more ants on the track than all the other teams put

together. The judges had made a special concession because ants are so small. However, when the ants brought their radish over the finishing line ahead of everyone else, some folks claimed that there were so many of them in the team that none of them had to do any running. They just passed the radish along the line.

The belly-flop competition was declared a 'no contest' and was awarded to the crocodiles. The other challengers had taken one look at the pond full of crocodiles and promptly retired.

The team of goldfish upheld the honor of the Big Tree with their win in the water polo event.

Garry Goldfish was the home team's top scorer.

At the end of the day, the medals were handed out. There were three gold medals for Big Tree competitors. Adam Ant accepted a medal on behalf of the ant's radish relay team, Garry Goldfish accepted one for the goldfish's water polo team, and Walter Woodpecker accepted one just for himself.

Before it was time to go home to baths and beds, Clarence Cat made a speech of thanks to the organizers. Then he advised everyone to begin training now, for next year's competition.

Molly and Morgan Mole were very much in love. Everyone expected them to get married and settle down to raising young moles at the Big Tree. But Morgan had dreams of life on the ocean and thrilling adventures. He was the sort of mole you might see in a port or a harbor anywhere in the world. One day, the call of the sea became too strong and Morgan set out to seek his fame and fortune.

He wrote to Molly every month and she treasured all his letters, sighing and crying over them. Each letter was mailed from a different port as Morgan's ship sailed around the world – until the vessel cast anchor at the Island of Molehills in the midst of the Velvet Sea. There Morgan found his paradise.

He settled down on the island, got himself a steady mining job, and bought an apartment.

Then he wrote to Molly, asking her to leave the Big Tree and come and join him.

Molly did not hesitate. She packed her warm weather clothes and gave away all the rest. She went around saying sad farewells to all her friends.

Dr. Mole was the only one on the jetty to see Molly sail away to join her Morgan on the Island of Molehills, but all the Big Tree residents wished her well with all their hearts, and thought that there was more romance in Molly and Morgan's story than in any book.

The Leaping, Laughing Envelopes

Every day, except Sundays, Frances Frog cycled around the neighborhood, delivering the mail. One fine morning, Big Tree folk were amazed to see the usually serious frog weaving about on her bicycle, her face red as she tried to stop herself from laughing out loud. Frances' mailbag was interfering with her! It kept bouncing about on her back, and trying to slip around to her front and tickle her tummy. Frances just couldn't control it.

The mailbag was very full that morning. It contained all the usual postcards, letters and packages. In addition, there were special, colored envelopes for the mailbox of every single apartment in the Big Tree. Frances' mailbag was behaving so improperly because all these colored envelopes were leaping and laughing.

The first animal in the Tree to open his colored envelope that morning was Bruce Bear, who had come out in his dressing gown and slippers to pick up the mail. As he opened the envelope, it burst out into a happy song, announcing the wedding of Louisa Lizard and Howie Hare and inviting the Bear family to the celebration.

Fiona Fox was the next to open her envelope. She was feeling tired but inspired. She had been typing her great novel all night long and was ready to go to bed now that it was morning. When she opened her dark blue envelope, it leapt out of her paws into the air. A shower of multi-colored dewdrops fell from it and formed the words: *Please*

come to the wedding of Louisa Lizard and Howie Hare.

When it was Walter Woodpecker's turn to open his envelope, he almost fell off his front branch. Out flew a cloud of bright yellow butterflies which danced around, spelling out his invitation to the happy occasion.

All over the Big Tree there were squeaks and squeals, growls and howls as happy folk opened their envelopes. Everyone was invited and everyone was determined to make Louisa and Howie's special day one which would never be forgotten by anyone at the Big Tree.

And so, when the sunny day dawned, everyone met in the clearing in front of the Tree. They were all dressed in their best clothes, to see the wedding of Louisa and Howie. Blushing a pretty shade of green, the bride wore a fairytale dress and Howie stood beside her looking handsome in his blue tuxedo. As the vows were spoken the youngsters threw flower petals over the happy couple, while the grown ups showed their joy by crying their eyes out!

The Poems of Daphne Duckling

Everyone at the Big Tree knew about Daphne Duckling and her passion for poetry. She spent hours each day in her nest by the pond writing poetry, and she could be seen swimming across the waters in all kinds of weather reciting her poems.

She wrote all her poems down in notebooks, which she sent off to Ducks and Drakes Inc., the famous publisher, in the hope that they would want to print them in a book. Unfortunately, nobody else could read Daphne's writing, because it isn't easy to write clearly if you have to hold your pen in a feathered wing.

One day, Daphne was at Fiona Fox's apartment, reading her latest poem out loud to her friend, who was listening so entranced that she ate all the cream cookies herself, without offering one to her guest. As Daphne reached the last line of her ballad about a duck and a dirty little duckling,

her voice broke: "... it made her sad to see her duck come home each night all covered in muck."

There was an outburst of cheering, mingled with sobs, from outside the window. There was an audience in the garden listening to Daphne's recital. Amongst them was the director of Big Tree Radio who immediately offered Daphne her own daily radio show 'Radio Rhymetime.'

And from then on, you would never see anyone near the Big Tree at three in the afternoon. Everyone was indoors listening to the radio, to the voice and poems of Daphne Duckling.

Saturday night at the Big Tree was dance night.

Every Saturday night, the lights went on near the Tree at The Velvet Paws Dance Hall. Over the entrance, the neon sign, flashing now green, now red, was visible all over the neighborhood.

Every Saturday night, through the swing ring doors of The Velvet Paws all the young, and not so young, Big Tree dance fans entered. In a chattering, cheerful throng dressed in their best clothes and dancing shoes they flocked into the hall.

Once inside, the animals who had come as couples sat together. The single animals gathered in corners opposite each other. The young males joked and laughed noisily and pushed each other around. The young females checked in the mirrors and made last minute adjustments to their fur or their feathers.

When the music started, the couples were always the first on the floor, moving together smoothly with the ease of long practice. The animals in the two corners moved towards each other, and there was always a bit of a scramble before everyone ended up with a partner. By then, the floor was packed with happy dancers.

The best dancer in the room was Captain Wolf, the brave chief of the firefighters. All the pretty young creatures who went to The Velvet Paws dreamed of dancing with him. Not only was he as handsome as a prince, but he also had good manners, and would always bow and kiss his partner's

paw or wing at the beginning and end of a dance.

One Saturday night, the dancing had already begun when Dinah Duck arrived at The Velvet Paws. Usually, Dinah was never seen there, but on

this occasion she had come to bring a warm, woolen scarf for a friend who had a cold.

As Dinah entered the dance hall, Captain Wolf caught sight of her and felt his heart beat faster. He had long worshiped the lovely duck from afar. What kind stroke of fate had brought her to him this evening?

Captain Wolf swept across the floor towards Dinah so he could be the first to ask her to dance. He brushed aside the darling duckling's protests and led her into the dance. Nobody had ever realized what a graceful and accomplished dancer she was!

It was a night for romance, and the love-smitten young couple danced together for the rest of the

evening. When the lights dimmed for the last time, Dinah curtsied and Captain Wolf kissed her wing in his usual gallant way. Together, through the moonlit woods, they walked home.

Orlando Owl's First Flight

Orlando Owl was ready to make his first flight. Preparations were being made at the Owls' nest.

Orlando's father, Oliver, had watched anxiously as he practiced take offs from a convenient molehill, and polished his landing techniques, "claws together, and roll sideways as you hit the ground."

His mother, Olga, had put together a traditional beginners' flying outfit – a made-to-measure, laurel leaf parachute, a padded flying jacket to prevent Orlando's feathers from getting ruffled, a half-acorn crash helmet and shatterproof, dark goggles so that he could see where he was going.

The great moment finally arrived. The little owl closed his eyes and jumped off his launching branch. Still keeping his eyes firmly shut, Orlando flapped his way straight into the clothesline on the Pandas' terrace! He opened his eyes, flapped his wings madly and swept upwards, leaving behind his parachute next to Pat Panda's shirts. He banged into the watch hanging from its branch on the Big Tree, then, in a daze, swung through Louisa Lizard's kitchen window and landed in a bowl of pudding.

It was then that Orlando, and everyone else, decided that he had done enough flying for one day. As he began to lick his feathers, Orlando felt that he thoroughly deserved this unexpected reward.

The Legendary Uncle

Little Mona Mouse loved writing letters. She wrote letters to all her relatives, to her friends, and she even wrote letters to young Willie, the Worm next door. To her great disappointment, she never got any replies. She said that the telephone was to blame. When someone received a letter from Mona, they immediately phoned to thank her and then there was nothing to write about!

But one day she did get a letter – from the legendary Uncle Ossie Ostrich. Everyone at the Big Tree knew about him, for he had been born there, but nobody had ever seen him. He had left the neighborhood at a very early age, and there had been nobody home in the Tree when he had made his only return visit.

Ossie's letter invited Mona to come and spend a

vacation with him at his sunny island nest. After thinking about it for a long time, Mr. and Mrs. Mouse agreed that Mona could go. They waved goodbye to her at the airport as she set off, with her flask of water over her shoulder and a bag full of cheese. They had heard about ostriches eating stones and didn't think the diet would agree with Mona.

After a month with Uncle Ossie, Mona returned

home. She had a suntanned tail and a head full of visions of sand dunes, and sailing ships, and mermaids. Uncle Ossie knew lots of mermaids.

"Show us photos of Uncle Ossie," asked all the Big Tree folk, who were desperate to see what he looked like. But, when Mona opened her case, out flew a cloud of blue butterflies, each one carrying a photo away with it. Walter Woodpecker caught a glimpse of some feathers. Olga Owl swore later that she had seen a beak. Monty Mouse said there was a top hat in a photo he had caught sight of. But Uncle Ossie remained a mystery, as the ocean is for those who have never seen it.

When the photos had fluttered away, nobody ever asked Mona to describe Ossie Ostrich to them. All the folks at the Big Tree felt the same way, that it was good for everyone to keep in their hearts and minds a small, private reserve, a mystery protected by blue butterflies!

It was Oliver Owl who thought of it first, probably because he was always reading, during his quiet hours as night watchman. Oliver told Bruce Bear. Bruce Bear told Walter Woodpecker, who told Cathy Crow, who told everybody.

As Sandy Squirrel painted such lovely pictures and Fiona Fox wrote such exciting stories, they were the ones who were asked to prepare the surprise for the youngsters – a book just for them, telling stories about the Big Tree and all the folks who lived in it.

So that they could work without being disturbed, Fiona and Sandy went off to the old abandoned tree trunk nearby. Sandy took his brushes and paints and drawing pad, and Fiona took her typewriter and typing paper. They were so caught up in their work that ideas for the stories and pictures came flying out of their heads as if by magic, and a bright spark would flash in the air above their heads with each one.

When everything was completed, they took their book back to the Big Tree. The youngsters

absolutely adored it. Arnold Ant read it right through without stopping. Betsy Bear couldn't stop looking at the pictures. Oscar Owl kept the

Big Tree book in bed with him under his pillow. The grown-up animals looked secretly at the

book. Walter Woodpecker checked through it to find out if Fiona had been true to life and had described him as handsome! Cathy Crow was offended and said that the crotchety bird in the book bore no resemblance to her at all. Oliver and Olga Owl took turns in reading the book aloud to each other. Captain Wolf climbed to the top of his long ladder and read it up there. From far away, Uncle Ossie sent a telegram of congratulations.

And every evening afterwards, as it grew dark, all over the woods you would find folks reading copies of *Goodnight Stories from the Big Tree*.

CONTENTS